CELEBRATION STORIES

A Present For Salima

KERENA

D1634309

Illustrated by Tim Clarey

W
HODDER
Wayland

an imprint of Hodder Children's Books

 # *A Special Time*

The Muslim month of Ramadan is a special time in the Islamic calendar. It was during this month hundreds of years ago that the angel Jibril recited the holy book, the Qur'an, to the Prophet Muhammad ﷺ.

Muslims remember this event by fasting during the whole month from first light in the morning until dusk in the evening. They spend their time reading the Qur'an and thinking about how God wants them to live their lives. It is also a time to think of others less well off than themselves.

A special night during Ramadan is the Night of Power. This falls towards the end of Ramadan. At this time, Muslims remember the night that the angel Jibril first recited the Qur'an to the Prophet Muhammad ﷺ. The Night of Power is marked in different ways all around the world. Special Ramadan prayers called *Tarawih* are said after dinner and may last all night.

In most celebrations reading the Qur'an aloud is an important part of the Night of Power.

The month of Ramadan begins with the new moon and ends when the next new moon brings the festival of Id-ul-Fitr. This festival marks the end of Ramadan and is celebrated by prayers, the giving of charity at the mosque, exchanging cards and gifts, and feasting. It's a time when Muslims feel closer to God and to other people after the Ramadan fast.

This story is set in Morocco, a Muslim country in North Africa. The events take place in the city of Taroudannt, an ancient, walled city that lies in an agricultural area of the country called the Sous Valley. The valley is bordered by the Atlas and mini Atlas Mountains.

Ibrahim

Ten-year-old Ibrahim stood high on the battlements of the ancient city of Taroudannt. He had lived here all his life, but he still loved the evening view. The sun was setting and the walls glowed golden. Beyond the walls Ibrahim could see orange and olive groves, tall date trees, and rushing streams.

Ibrahim could see his parents' farm and their garden. And he could just make out his mother and his little sister, picking the vegetables that his father would sell in the market the next day.

Right in the distance were the mountains. Ibrahim had never been that far away from home.

He wondered what it was like to live somewhere that wasn't flat. He had seen some of the men who lived there come to market to sell their leather goods. They didn't wear modern, western clothes like Ibrahim and his father, they wore the old-style long robes of Morocco.

Towering above Ibrahim, on the minaret of the city mosque, the muezzin started to call people to prayer.

"God is great! God is great!" he cried. "There is no God but Allah."

The muezzin's call reminded Ibrahim of his faith. He was a Muslim. He went to a school at the mosque where he learned Arabic so that he could read and recite the Qur'an.

Ibrahim knew that he should stop and pray, but he was late for his evening's work.

He climbed down from the battlements and made his way to the central square. He didn't stop at the mosque where the worshippers were by now coming out. He went straight into the souk, the covered market.

The souk was crowded as usual. Ibrahim
passed stalls selling spices and dried flowers,
sandals and clothes. Shoppers bartered with
stallholders, hoping to get a bargain. There were
several people at his father's stall buying fresh
marrow, quince, potatoes and aubergines. But
Ibrahim couldn't stop to help his father. He had
his own job in the souk.

11

"You're late," complained Mustafa, the old tea seller.

There was no time for excuses. Ibrahim quickly took the brass tray with rows of glasses of hot mint tea from Mustafa.

"Take these teas before they get cold," ordered the old man.

Ibrahim carried the tray to each of the
stallholders, who paid for their tea with a coin.
When the tray was empty, Ibrahim returned to
Mustafa for more tea. When the glasses ran out,
he had to rush around the stalls to collect the
used ones and wash them.

Ibrahim worked really hard. It was late at
night when the stallholders finally packed up
and Ibrahim could go home with his father.

The New Moon

Ibrahim fetched the horse and cart. His father loaded up all the vegetables he hadn't sold on to the cart while Ibrahim lit the lantern. Then his father drove them down the narrow lanes, through the gates of the city and out into the countryside.

14

The lantern was old and its light was dim. It was difficult to see the path. There were no street lamps in the city or lights on the tracks that led to the farm. Ibrahim's father seemed excited about something. He kept looking up at the moon.

"What do you see in the sky, Ibrahim?" he asked.

"Just the moon," replied Ibrahim, puzzled.

"It's the *new* moon," his father explained. "When the new moon comes it's a new month. And now it's the month of Ramadan."

Ibrahim peered at the moon shining behind the black battlements of Taroudannt. Over the next month it would grow fatter and become a full moon, then finally a new moon again. During that time the grown-ups would fast from first light until dusk. When the next new moon arrived, the month of Ramadan would end and then it would be the festival of Id-ul-Fitr.

Ibrahim loved Id. It was a holiday, so nobody worked. In the square by the mosque there were snake charmers, acrobats and fire-eaters. Families gave each other presents and cards. Ibrahim couldn't wait! He decided that every night he would watch the moon to see when the festival would come.

 # Ramadan Begins

The next day the family awoke before first light. They began their breakfast with prayers and ate dates gathered from the tree in the garden. After breakfast Ibrahim and his father loaded the fresh vegetables on to the cart and began their journey to the souk.

By the time they reached Taroudannt it was dawn and the muezzin was chanting from the mosque, "Come to prayer. Come to prayer. Prayer is better than sleep."

When they arrived at the mosque, Ibrahim and his father washed and went in to pray.

Then they made their way to the souk and set up the vegetable stall. It was a hot day and Ibrahim was thankful that the souk was covered.

Once he had helped his father, Ibrahim went to find Mustafa. But when he reached the place where the old tea seller usually sat, Mustafa wasn't there.

Ibrahim wondered where he could be. It was hot in the souk and Ibrahim was sure that the stallholders would like a refreshing drink of tea.

He also hoped that if he sold lots of tea he could save

some extra money to buy Id presents for his family.

Ibrahim's father called out to him. "If you're looking for Mustafa, you won't find him until this evening when we break our fast. Nobody will drink tea during the day."

Of course! Ibrahim had forgotten. The grown-ups did not eat during the day and they didn't drink either, not even tea or water. Ibrahim suddenly thought how difficult fasting must be in the hot weather.

"Aren't you thirsty, Father?" he asked.

"I don't think about it. When customers come I serve them. And when there are no customers I recite what is written in the Qur'an. I don't have time to think about being thirsty."

Ibrahim looked around the souk. It was normally so busy. Today it was peaceful. The stallholders seemed thoughtful and the few customers didn't spend as long driving bargains. Ibrahim wondered what it would be like to fast. Children weren't supposed to fast, but maybe he could.

"Father, I would like to fast," he declared.

His father looked at him proudly.

Ibrahim felt very grown-up. "I want to know what it's like to fast and the only way to find out is to do it myself," he added.

"Very well," his father replied, smiling. "You shall have one day when you will eat nothing. But you should drink some water – it's bad for children not to drink."

Ibrahim was really excited.

Ibrahim's Fast

One morning, when the family woke up, well before daybreak, Ibrahim's father announced, "Today Ibrahim is going to fast."

Ibrahim felt important. He wanted to refuse his breakfast but his mother encouraged him to eat and drink more than usual. She even made him eat a whole plate of dates.

"The sugar in those dates will keep you going," she told him.

That day Ibrahim's father didn't load up the cart for the souk. Instead, he took Ibrahim on a long walk up to the main road, where they sat and waited.

Soon a van drove up with some of the stallholders inside. Ibrahim and his father climbed in.

Ibrahim had never travelled in a van before. He was so excited! "Where are we going, Father?" he asked.

"We're driving to the mountains to get rugs, shoes and belts so that we can sell them as Id presents in the market."

Ibrahim could not believe it! He was finally going to see what the mountains were like. It was turning out to be a very special day indeed.

Peering through the van window, Ibrahim could see the distant mountains getting closer all the time. It began to get hotter as the sun climbed higher and higher in the sky. Ibrahim was thirsty and wanted a drink, but there was no water in the van. He could see the streams running  beside the road but he didn't want to ask to stop. He knew that the other men couldn't drink. He would feel bad if they had to watch him drinking.

So Ibrahim began to see how many verses of the Qur'an he could remember in his head, and he soon forgot about his thirst.

 # In the Mountains

The road became more bumpy as the van climbed into the mountains. There were no more streams and date trees, no orange and olive groves. Instead, all Ibrahim could see were rocks on stony ground and a few prickly trees. Ibrahim looked more closely at the trees. There was something strange about them. High up on the branches there were large dark shapes. And they were moving!

"Look at those trees!" he shouted. "There are big moving things growing on the branches!"

Everybody laughed and the van stopped.

"Go and take a closer look, Ibrahim," said his father, his eyes twinkling.

Ibrahim jumped out of the van and ran towards the strange trees. Then he saw what the black shapes were. Goats! On all the branches of the trees! Ibrahim's goat at home never climbed trees to find food – it ate vegetable scraps.

He looked at the stony ground under his feet. No wonder the goats ate the prickly trees – no other plants could grow in the soil here. He wondered where the goats got water from. Thinking about water made Ibrahim thirsty again.

When he got back in the van his father said, "We'll stop at the next village and you can get some water there." After a while the van slowed to a halt at a small village called Tichka.

Ibrahim got out of the van and looked around. The houses here were different from his house. They were more like stone huts. He could see straight away that there was no stream, no well, and no shops. He would have to ask for water at one of the houses.

"Can I help you?" a voice asked. It was a young girl.

"I'd like a drink of water," Ibrahim replied.

"Follow me," said the girl. "My name is Salima."

Salima led Ibrahim along a path up the mountain. It was very steep and Ibrahim's legs were beginning to ache. He was soon puffing and panting and his throat felt really dry.

"Are you sure there's water here?" he gasped.

"Of course! I climb up here to get water every day," replied Salima, marching quickly ahead.

After more climbing they finally came to a small cave. Salima went in and Ibrahim followed.

It was dark inside and Ibrahim stumbled on some rocks and fell over. His knee hurt and he was scared, but he didn't want to cry in front of Salima.

"Kneel down and lean over this rock," said Salima. "If you cup your hands you can get some water from the stream."

At first it was difficult to find the water in
the dark. Ibrahim felt a small trickle of water
and scooped up some in his hands. He drank a
mouthful, scooped again and drank some more.
He still felt thirsty, but he didn't want to drink
too much as there was only a little water in
the stream.

"This is the only way we can get water in our village," Salima explained. "Every day we climb up to the cave. It would be much easier if we had candles but we can't afford them."

Ibrahim couldn't believe how difficult it was for Salima and the other villagers to get water. All he had to do was go to a stream, or buy a bottle from a shop, or use the well. He hadn't realized how lucky he was.

Ibrahim was quiet all the way back to the van. There had to be something he could do to help Salima. Then he had an idea. He could give her some candles for Id!

But there was just one problem – candles were very expensive.

As the van drove off, Ibrahim spent the rest of the journey thinking about how he could raise enough money to buy his special present.

 # The Night of Power

A few days later it was the Night of Power. Ibrahim's parents were dressed in their best clothes. Ibrahim and his sister were going to take part in a procession with the children of Taroudannt, so they wore special clothes, too.

But Ibrahim was in no mood for celebrating. He couldn't stop thinking about Salima and the villagers of Tichka. He had saved some money to buy Id presents for his family, but there wasn't enough left to buy even one candle.

It was evening when Ibrahim's family arrived in the city for the celebrations. Outside the mosque a drummer beat a large drum. Ibrahim's father joined the group of men going into the mosque. They would remain there all night reciting the Qur'an aloud.

Ibrahim and his sister joined the children who were waiting to march round the city in the procession. There would soon be a new moon and Ramadan would end. Then the celebration of Id would begin. Ibrahim didn't have much time to earn enough money to buy candles.

At that moment the dark battlements were lit and all of the children were given torches, lanterns and lamps to carry along in the procession.

"Here, take this." Someone nudged Ibrahim and handed him a candle.

Ibrahim couldn't believe it! Now he had one candle to give to the villagers of Tichka!

He put the candle in his bag. Surely it
wouldn't matter if he didn't carry a light.

Ibrahim followed in the procession and
collected up any candles that had burnt down.
Soon he had a bag full of candle stumps. He
could melt down the wax to make one large
new candle. Then he would have the perfect
present for Salima's village!

 The Id Moon Comes

Ibrahim stood on the battlements of Taroudannt watching the moon rise in the sky, as he had done every night of Ramadan.

It was a new moon! The festival of Id-ul-Fitr had come!

The next morning at first light Ibrahim and his family went to the mosque for prayers and the traditional giving of charity. Only after that could they give out their cards and presents. Ibrahim carried the candle he had made for Salima in his bag. But the mountains were so far away. How could he give the present to her?

After prayers everyone gathered in the square to celebrate Id. All around the square there were food stalls. Musicians played drums, flutes, and *guenbris.* There were snake charmers, storytellers, fire-eaters, acrobats and clowns.

Ibrahim didn't join in the celebrations because Mustafa was so busy. Everyone wanted tea, and Ibrahim went to help.

"Are you going to the village of Tichka?" he asked his customers, hopefully.

But each one said, "No."

Ibrahim felt he had asked every person in the square. Nobody could help him.

As the celebrations were ending, Ibrahim's father came up to him.

"I have your Id present," he announced, smiling, and handed Ibrahim the lantern from their cart. "I've seen you collecting candles," he said. "The lantern will give a much better light. I'll get a new one for the cart."

It was perfect! Now Ibrahim had a wonderful present for Salima and the villagers. But he still had no way of getting it to them. It was useless. He looked down at the lantern and sighed.

"What's the matter?"asked his father. "Don't you like your present?"

Ibrahim told him all about Salima and the villagers of Tichka, and why he had been collecting candles.

His father smiled warmly. "I'm proud of you, Ibrahim," he said. "You have followed the teachings of the Qur'an and have truly thought of others. I know one of the traders from that village. I'll ask him to take your present there for you."

Ibrahim was overjoyed! Whenever he looked at the mountains he would think of the villagers climbing up the hill to get water with his lantern to light up the cave.

Glossary

Allah Allah is the Arabic word for God.

Angel Jibril Also known as Gabriel. It was Jibril who recited the Qur'an to the Prophet Muhammad ﷺ.

Fast To go without food or drink.

Guenbris A traditional Moroccan musical instrument that looks like a long guitar.

Id-ul-Fitr The festival that comes after the Ramadan fast. It is also one of the two most important Muslim festivals and the first day of the month of Shawwal.

Minaret The long, thin, tower of a mosque where the muezzin stand to do the call to prayer.

Morocco A country in North Africa.

Muezzin A person who chants the call to prayer from the minaret of a mosque.

Night of Power The twenty-sixth night of Ramadan, when the angel Jibril recited the Qur'an to the Prophet Muhammad ﷺ.

Prophet Muhammad ﷺ The Prophet Muhammad ﷺ was the Prophet of Islam. It was to him that God revealed the Qur'an.

Souk The Arabic word for market. The souk is usually near the mosque.

Qur'an The Muslims' holy book. It tells them how to live a good life. It is written in rhythmic text in a language called Arabic.

Ramadan A month in the Islamic calendar. During this month grown-ups and children over twelve years of age fast from first light to dusk.

CELEBRATION STORIES

Look out for these other titles in the **Celebration Stories** series:

The Dragon Doorway by Clare Bevan
Nothing's going right for Nathan's family – Dad's broken his big toe, the roof's leaking, and Mum's lost her pantomime job as Goldy the Magic Chicken… So when a competition leaflet comes through the door, promising a family ticket for a mystery tour, Nathan thinks it's worth a try. All he's got to do is solve a riddle. But no one seems to have a clue – until Nathan finds the Dragon Doorway…

The Treasure of Santa Cruz by Saviour Pirotta
Salvador can't believe his luck. He's always wanted to carry the cross of Santa Cruz in the Good Friday pageant and now he's been chosen. It's a dream come true. But then tragedy strikes and Salvador is asked to let his friend Juan take his place. How can Salvador sacrifice something he's wanted for his whole life?

Waiting For Elijah by Ann Jungman
Debbie has always asked the four questions at the Passover meal – it's her favourite part. So when she finds out that her younger cousin will be doing it this year, Debbie's upset. Worse still, she has to open the door to the Prophet Elijah instead – and he never comes. But then a new friend helps her to realize that opening the door to Elijah is more important than she thinks.

You can buy all these books from your local bookseller, or order them direct from the publisher. For more information about Celebration Stories, write to: *The Sales Department, Hodder Children's Books, a division of Hodder Headline Limited, 338 Euston Road, London NW1 3BH.*